P9-DMA-875

This book belongs to

Michelle, Elijah, and Sonny, with love

G.P.-P.

This edition published by Parragon Books Ltd in 2013 and distributed by
Parragon Inc.
440 Park Avenue South, 13th Floor
New York, NY 10016
www.parragon.com

Published by arrangement with Gullane Children's Books

Text © Giles Paley-Phillips 2013
Illustrations © Liz Pichon 2013

All rights reserved. No part of this publication may be reproduced, stored in a retrieval
system or transmitted, in any form or by any means, electronic, mechanical, photocopying,
recording or otherwise, without the prior permission of the copyright holder.

ISBN 978-1-4723-3594-4

Printed in China

# THINGS YOU NEVER KNEW About
# DINOSAURS

Giles
Paley-Phillips

illustrated by
Liz Pichon

PaRragon

Bath · New York · Singapore · Hong Kong · Cologne · Delhi
Melbourne · Amsterdam · Johannesburg · Shenzhen

Did you know that dinosaurs
Are still around today?
They didn't die off long ago,
They never went away.

On every street in every town,
Maybe next door to you,
Dinosaurs are doing things
You won't BELIEVE are true...

Dinosaurs play tennis.

They ride around on bikes.

They
like
to
bounce
on
trampolines . . .

and go for hilltop hikes.

Dinosaurs love to play guitar,

To stomp their feet and sing.

They love to waltz and
cha cha cha
And do the Highland fling.

There are some things they DON'T like much,
Things they really HATE!
Dinosaurs don't like doing math . . .

or always having to wait!

You'll never see them brush their teeth
Or clean their dirty plates.
And when they should be fast asleep,
They're whizzing around on skates!

Some dinosaurs go up in space
To see the Moon and Mars.

Others go to Hollywood
And become big movie stars.

Dinosaurs sail the seven seas,

They trek from pole to pole . . .

And in the World Cup final
One scored the **winning goal.**

GO PTERODACTYL!

Yes, dinosaurs do amazing things,
It's all completely true.
But most of all,
their favorite thing . . .